Judy Moody
and the Bad Luck Charm

Megan McDonald is the award-winning author of the Judy Moody series. She says that most of Judy's stories "grew out of anecdotes about growing up with my four sisters". She confesses, "I am Judy Moody. Same-same! In my family of sisters, we're famous for exaggeration. Judy Moody is me ... exaggerated." Megan McDonald lives with her husband in northern California.

You can find out more about Megan McDonald and her books at **www.meganmcdonald.net**

Peter H. Reynolds says he felt an immediate connection to Judy Moody because "having a daughter, I have witnessed first-hand the adventures of a very independent-minded girl". Peter H. Reynolds lives in Massachusetts, just down the road from his twin brother.

You can find out more about Peter H. Reynolds and his art at **www.fablevision.com**

Books by Megan McDonald and Peter H. Reynolds

Judy Moody
Judy Moody Gets Famous!
Judy Moody Saves the World!
Judy Moody Predicts the Future
Judy Moody: The Doctor Is In!
Judy Moody Declares Independence!
Judy Moody: Around the World in 8½ Days
Judy Moody Goes to College
Judy Moody, Girl Detective
Judy Moody and the NOT Bummer Summer
Stink: The Incredible Shrinking Kid
Stink and the Incredible Super-Galactic Jawbreaker
Stink and the World's Worst Super-Stinky Sneakers
Stink and the Great Guinea Pig Express
Stink: Solar System Superhero
Stink and the Ultimate Thumb-Wrestling Smackdown
Stink and the Midnight Zombie Walk
Stink-O-Pedia: Super Stink-y Stuff from A to Zzzzz
Stink-O-Pedia 2: More Stink-y Stuff from A to Z
Judy Moody & Stink: The Holly Joliday
Judy Moody & Stink: The Mad, Mad, Mad, Mad Treasure Hunt

Books by Megan McDonald

Ant and Honey Bee: What a Pair!
The Sisters Club
The Sisters Club: Rule of Three
The Sisters Club: Cloudy with a Chance of Boys

Books by Peter H. Reynolds

The Dot • Ish • So Few of Me

Judy ody

and the charm

Megan McDonald

illustrated by

Peter H. Reynolds

WALKER
BOOKS

First published in Great Britain 2013 by Walker Books Ltd
87 Vauxhall Walk, London SE11 5HJ

2 4 6 8 10 9 7 5 3 1

Text © 2012 Megan McDonald
Illustrations © 2012 Peter H. Reynolds
Judy Moody font © 2003 Peter H. Reynolds

This book has been typeset in Stone Informal

Printed and bound in Great Britain by Clays Ltd, St Ives plc

British Library Cataloguing in Publication Data:
a catalogue record for this book
is available from the British Library

ISBN 978-1-4063-4419-6

www.walker.co.uk

For Jordan and Chloe, my good-luck charms
M. M.

To my talented pal Megan McDonald
P. H. R.

Table of Contents

Judy Moody

Be-charmed
third-grade pig sitter;
Queen of the Growlery

Who's

Dad

Spelling-list rescuer

Mom

Road-trip mastermind

Stink

Prize Claw timekeeper
and fellow pig sitter

Who

ROCKY

Best friend and
no. 1 study buddy

Frank

Floater in the Moater
bowler buddy

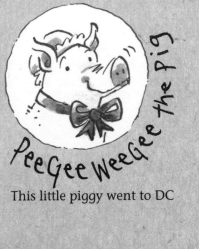

PeeGee WeeGee the Pig

This little piggy went to DC

Jessica

*Very berry cherry funny
money* super speller

The Lucky Penny

She, Judy Moody, had a penny. Not just any penny. Not a regular old Abe Lincoln penny.

A lucky penny. No lie!

Judy and her family took Grandma Lou out to breakfast at the Two Chicks on a Raft Diner. Stink ordered – what else? – silver-dollar pancakes. Judy said, "I'll have the special – two chicks on a raft. And some moo juice."

"Moo juice?" asked Stink, sitting up.

Judy pointed to all the funny names for food on the menu. "Two eggs on toast. And milk to drink."

"Chocolate moo for me, please," said Stink.

"So anyway," Judy told her family, "Grandma Lou took me roller-skating at Mount Trashmore, right?"

"And we rolled right past one of those penny machines," said Grandma Lou.

"And she gave me this way-old penny she had from the 1970s—"

"Waayy old," said Grandma Lou, smiling.

"And we put it in the machine and – check it out!" Judy held up a penny with a four-leaf clover

inside a horseshoe that said MY LUCKY PENNY. MT. TRASHMORE, VA.

"That's not a lucky penny," said Stink. "That's a squashed penny. Weird. It looks like it got run over."

"It's still a lucky penny, Stink," said Judy. "Says so right on it, see?"

"How much did you pay for that?" Stink asked.

"Fifty-one cents," said Judy.

"Fifty-one cents! You paid fifty-one cents for a penny?"

"A *lucky* penny," said Judy.

"It's a special penny," said Mum. "A keepsake."

"A souvenir," said Dad.

"I'm so going to start collecting these,"

said Judy, rubbing her penny. "It'll be my new thing."

"I thought your new thing was collecting banana stickers," said Stink. "And ice-lolly sticks with jokes on them."

"Stink? Do you have to know everything about me?"

"Kids," Dad warned. "Don't start."

While they waited for their food, Judy got an idea. She had seen a machine in the front lobby. A way-cool machine full of something else she collected. Stuffed animals!

"Grandma Lou?" Judy asked. "Do you have any quarters?"

Grandma Lou dug down to the bottom of her purse. "Four. Will that do?"

"Yes. Thanks, Grandma Lou!"

"Are you gonna smash quarters, too?" Stink asked.

"No, I just want to play the Super Claw," said Judy. She pointed to the glass case.

"Forget it," said Stink. "It's super-impossible. Nobody beats The Claw!"

"Yah-huh," said Judy. "People do. Or else the glass case would be full. Besides, it's fun to try. What's there to lose?"

"Duh! Money!"

Judy scooped up the quarters. "C'mon, Stink-o. Before the food gets here."

She dashed away from the table and headed for the lobby.

"Wait for me!" said Stink.

"One, two, three..." Judy said. "We have exactly four quarters."

"It costs a dollar a turn!" said Stink. "That's four quarters."

"I'll go first," said Judy.

"But then I get to go *never*," said Stink.

"Not if I win. If I win, we get a free turn," said Judy.

"Like I said. Never," said Stink.

"C'mon, Stink," said Judy, pressing her nose to the glass. "Which one should we go for?"

"The yellow elephant," said Stink. "His ear's sticking up. No wait. The blue monkey! No wait! The green lion."

"Purple rhino it is!" said Judy. *Clinkety-clink-clink-clink!* The four quarters landed in the machine. *Whirr!* The thirty seconds began ticking away. Judy grabbed the joystick. She moved the giant arm until the claw dangled right over the purple rhino.

"Hurry up!" said Stink, standing on tiptoes to see better. "You only have twenty-three more seconds."

She, Judy Moody, went in for the big grab.

Stink leaned in closer. "Six seconds!" he said.

The open tentacles of the claw came down around the rhino's snout. "Gotcha!" Judy whispered. She pressed the big green button on the joystick to lock the claw in place.

"Don't drop him!" shouted Stink.

Judy held her breath. She tried not to itch. She tried not to twitch. *Steady, steady. Careful, careful.* With the joystick, she eased the rhino over to the chute and *wa la*! She let go. He slid down the chute into the hatch.

Judy opened the prize door and pulled out the purple rhino. "Mine, all mine!" she cooed, hugging it to her.

"Free turn," said Stink. "I'm next."

"No way, Stinker."

"But you said—"

"Stink, I won! I beat The Claw! I'm on a roll. Do you really want to mess with that kind of luck?"

Stink shook his head no.

Judy reached into her pocket and rubbed her lucky penny. "Ready?" she asked.

Stink nodded. "Ready, Freddy," he said.

Judy took hold of the joystick. Her hand was sweating. She took a deep breath.

"Orange cow," said Stink, pointing. "Go for the orange cow!"

In just under seventeen seconds, Judy managed to nab the orange cow, keep it in the grip of the claw and send it down the chute to the prize door.

"We won," said Stink, reaching in first to grab the orange cow. "You did it. You beat The Claw two times in a row!"

"Free turn," said the machine. "Free turn."

"Should we go for three?" Judy asked.

"Yeah, yeah, yeah-yeah-yeah," said Stink. He was so excited his cheeks flushed bright red.

"OK, Stinker. Your turn. The pressure is on."

"No way!" said Stink. "You're on a crazy good winning streak."

Judy took out her lucky penny and set it on the machine. "C'mon, lucky penny," she whispered. She clutched the joystick one more time.

This time, she grabbed a blue monkey – barely – by the tip of the tippy tail. She pulled back on the joystick, slowly, slowly.

"Don't drop it!" said Stink. "You're going to drop it."

Blue Monkey's head bumped into Pink Crab's claw!

"Watch out!" said Stink.

At last, Judy let go of the button and Blue Monkey dropped down into the prize chute. Music went off. Lights blinked and flashed. "Game over!" said the machine.

Judy and Stink rushed back to their

table, clutching Purple Rhino, Orange Cow and Blue Monkey.

"Whoa," said Stink. "You beat The Claw three times in a row! That's like some kind of record."

Judy held up her shiny coin and smiled. "It's all because of my lucky penny, of course!" she said.

Good Luck x 3

The next day, three things happened to Judy. Three good-luck things.

Judy woke up just like she did on any other normal old day. She ran downstairs to eat breakfast just like she did on any other normal old day.

"Stink, pass the Lucky Os, please."

Stink passed the cereal. Judy poured Lucky Os into her bowl. She added milk.

That's when it happened. Good-Luck Thing Number One.

One, two, three, four, five, six, seven fun-shaped marshmallows floated in her cereal. "Stink! Check it out! How many marshmallows do you see?"

Stink counted. "Seven?"

"Exactly! Seven is a lucky number. In fact, seven is the luckiest number of all."

"Can I eat a lucky marshmallow?" Stink reached his spoon towards her bowl.

Judy swatted his hand away. "No! I have to see if any of these are purple horseshoes. Horseshoes are super lucky."

Judy reached in and plucked out a purple horseshoe. "It's a double!" she squealed. "Two purple horseshoes stuck together. Double stuff is lucky, too."

Stink looked in his bowl. He looked in the box. But he did not see any more double lucky marshmallows. "You have all the luck," said Stink.

He put a spoonful of *un*-lucky cereal in his mouth. He slumped down in his chair to chew. Suddenly, his eyes stopped blinking and his whole body froze.

"What? What's wrong?" Judy asked.

"My lucky ketchup packet!" said Stink, with a mouthful of half-chewed cereal. "I sat on it."

"Huh?"

"Yesterday at the diner, when you had a lucky penny in your pocket, I wanted a lucky thing, too. So I put a ketchup packet in my back pocket for *my* lucky thing.

But I forgot about it and I think I just smooshed it." Stink made a scrunched-up, I-just-sat-on-ketchup face.

"Ooh, ick. Let me see!" said Judy.

Stink stood up and wiped his trousers with his hands. Sure enough, there was ketchup smeared all over his trousers. There was ketchup smooshed all over the chair.

Judy handed Stink a dishcloth. "Here, wipe up the ketchup volcano."

She closed up the cereal box. Ouch! Paper cut! (Bad luck.) But a paper cut meant she got to wear a Band-Aid! (Good luck.)

Judy ran upstairs and took out her Crazy Strips collection. She had eyeball bandages, zombies and crime-scene tape ones. Rainbows, sushi, nesting dolls. Toast!

She shook out all the toast-shaped bandages and wrapped one around her finger. Wait just a peanut-butter-and-jam minute! What's this? A folded-up wad of ... dollar bills!

Ten whole dollars! What were they doing in the box of Crazy Strips? Maybe Stink hid them and forgot about them.

Who cares! She was rich!

Judy origami-folded each dollar bill into a ring. A money ring! One for each finger. Good-Luck Thing Number Two.

☙ ☙ ☙

That afternoon, Judy Moody, Blue Monkey, Purple Rhino and ten lucky dollars got dropped off at Jessica Finch's birthday bowling party at Starlight Lanes. When she got inside, Judy raced around the lobby looking for a Super Claw machine.

"Are you looking for us?" asked Frank and Rocky, coming up beside her. Frank pointed to a lane in the far corner where the Finches were bowling. Jessica Finch waved. "We're over there."

"First I was looking for a Super Claw machine," Judy told her friends. She showed them Purple Rhino and Blue Monkey. She told them about her good-luck streak. She held out her hands. Each finger had a money ring. Ten dollars = ten tries to beat the Super Claw! "I could win ten tons of stuffed animals," Judy said.

Rocky and Frank raced around after her, looking too.

"No Super Claw machine," said Rocky.

"No Super Claw machine," said Frank.

Bummeroo.

Jessica Finch ran up to them. "Hi, Judy! Can you believe I get a bowling party for my birthday? C'mon, guys! The Xtreme Bowling Challenge is about to begin." The kids rushed back to the far lane.

"Hi, Mr and Mrs Finch," said Judy.

"Hey, kiddo," said Mr Finch. "Glad you could make it."

"Love your bowling-pin leggings," said Mrs Finch, smiling.

"Thanks!" said Judy.

All of a sudden, the lights went down. Music came over the loudspeakers. Neon-bright coloured lights flickered and flashed on the bowling lanes.

"Rare!" said Judy.

A voice came over the sound system. "It's time – Xtreme Bowling time – for people who like to knock stuff down!"

Everybody cheered.

"As you know, each bowler gets three balls. And the goal is to get not one, not two, but three strikes in a row."

"Whoa," said Frank.

A guy dressed as a bowling pin came over to their lane. "Are you, Birthday Girl Jessica Finch, ready to rock the Xtreme

Challenge?" he yelled into the mike.

"Yes!" she screamed.

"Let's get this par-tee star-ted!" said the human bowling pin.

Other bowlers gathered around to watch. "Go, Jessica!" everybody yelled.

Jessica Finch rolled her first ball down the lane. "Baby Ball!" said the human bowling pin. He used funny names like Big Ears and Snake Eyes for bowling moves.

"Try again," the guy said.

Jessica rolled the second ball.

"Powder Puff! Sorry. Not hard enough. Once more for the B-day girl."

Jessica rolled a third ball.

"A 3-6-10 split. That's what we call a Poison Ivy. Not bad, but sorry, no cigar."

Rocky took the Xtreme Challenge next.

"Will he choke?" asked the human bowling pin. Rocky's first ball hit three pins. His second ball hit five pins. On Rocky's third try, the guy yelled, "Blowout!

All but one. So close."

Frank Pearl took the Xtreme Challenge next.

"Try Number One. Creeper! Try Number Two. Sleeper! Try Number Three. Floater in the Moater! That means gutter ball, folks. Next!"

At last it was Judy's turn. She stepped up to the lane. She rubbed her lucky penny. She rubbed the bowling ball. She held it in front of her, lining it up. She squinted one eye, pulled back her arm and let it fly.

"Lookin' good, lookin' good, lookin'– STEE-rike!" yelled the human bowling pin. "We have a winner! But can she do it again?"

Judy bowled a second ball.

"Double-double! Super strike!" yelled the guy. "This one's on a lucky streak. Can the girl in the I ATE A SHARK T-shirt make it three in a row? Or will it be a dead apple in the gutter?"

Judy bowled a third ball. It leaned left. It leaned right. It picked up speed, straightened up and *KA-BOOM*! All ten pins toppled like a house of sugar packets.

Neon lights flashed. A horn blared. Everybody crowded around went cuckoo.

"And we have a Turkey!" yelled the guy.

"A Turkey? But I knocked down all the pins!" said Judy.

Mr and Mrs Finch laughed.

"A turkey means *three* strikes in a row." The human bowling pin took Judy's arm and held it in the air like a prizefighter. "Didn't this girl just BOWL you over, folks?" The crowd went wild. The human bowling pin bobbed his head in a turkey dance. "Gobble, gobble, gobble." The human bowling pin turned a cartwheel across three lanes. "Congrats, Shark Girl. Your name goes on the Bowling Pin Wall of Fame."

"Wow!" said Jessica.

"Double wow!" said Rocky.

"Triple wow!" said Frank.

"That was really something," said Mrs Finch.

"Glow sticks for everyone at the birthday girl's party!" said the guy. "And a blow-up bowling pin for the birthday girl."

"Thanks!" said Jessica.

"Let's get those birthday treats up here. And don't forget the cake!"

While they munched on mac-and-cheese bites and pretzel dippers, Jessica said, "Judy? Will you sign my bowling pin?"

Judy signed her autograph on Jessica's bowling pin. In cursive.

"You sure are lucky," said Jessica.

"All we got was one Christmas Tree, a Poison Ivy and a bunch of gutter balls," said Frank. "I mean Poodle Puffs. I mean Powder Puffs."

"Huh?" said Rocky.

"Whatever. You know. Funny names, like the bowling pin guy uses. Poison Ivy is a 3-6-10 split. And Christmas Tree is a 3-7-10 split."

"I owe it all to my lucky penny," said Judy. She held it up and kissed it.

"*Lucky* is your middle name," said Frank.

"Just call me Judy 'Lucky' Moody," said Judy.

Planet Lucky

At inside break on Monday morning, Frank asked Judy, "Do you think something lucky will happen to you at school today?"

"Sure. Why not?" said Judy.

"Like what?" asked Rocky.

"Like ... maybe I'll find my missing *Clue of the Broken Locket* library book or

Frank will give me back my Grouchy pencil."

"Oops," said Frank, fishing around inside his desk.

"Or I'll get picked to take Peanut home this weekend. Or Mr Todd will cancel our spelling test."

"Yeah, right," said Rocky. "The only thing that would cancel a spelling test is if lightning struck the school, it caught on fire and we all had to run out of the building."

Just then, Mr Todd blinked the lights. "Settle down, class. Let's get back to work."

Mr Todd leaned against his desk. "Instead of a spelling test today—"

"I knew it!" Judy blurted.

"Whoa. This *is* your lucky day!" Frank whispered.

"Excuse me?" said Mr Todd. "Am I going to have to get out the Interrupting Jar again?"

"Sorry," said Judy, zipping her lips.

"As I was saying, instead of a spelling test today, we're going to have a practice spelling bee. As you all know, our class spelling bee is coming up in a week. Whoever wins will get to go with the winners from the other third-grade classes at Virginia Dare School to take part in the Great Third-Grade Spelling Bee at the end of the month."

"Everybody knows Jessica Finch is the WBS," said Judy.

"WBS?" said Mr Todd, wrinkling his forehead.

"World's Best Speller," said Judy.

"You never know," said Mr Todd. "If you try hard enough, you could be the lucky speller who gets to represent Class 3T in Washington DC."

Washington DC! As in home of the president and the Museum of Doctor Stuff and the giant giant's head sticking up out of the ground? As in the same exact place where Stink got to go to the White House and she didn't?

She, Judy Moody, could not believe her lucky-ducky ears. She could not bite her *un*-interrupting tongue for one more second.

Judy raised her hand. "Excuse me, Mr Todd. Did you say Washington DC?"

"Yes," said Mr Todd. "The Great Third-Grade Spelling Bee will be held at our sister school, Orchard Elementary, in Washington DC."

"Did you know that's where the White House is?" Judy asked.

"I am aware of that, yes," said Mr Todd, smiling.

"Well, did you know they also have the Museum of Doctor Stuff with a for-real Abraham Lincoln bone?"

"I did not know that," said Mr Todd. "Very interesting."

"It is," said Judy. "They have an actual hunk of his skull. No lie."

"Ooh! Gross!" said the other kids in the class.

"Who knows? Maybe you'll get a

chance to see it." Mr Todd stood up and rubbed his hands together. "OK, Class 3T. Are you ready for our practice bee? All the words are from the study sheets you've been working on these last few weeks. When I call your name, please come up to the front and face the class. Spell your word and use it in a sentence, please."

Judy Moody could not keep her mind on spelling. All she could think about was how much she wanted to go to Washington DC. DC was for Definitely Cool!

If only she didn't have to *spell* to get there.

Then Judy remembered. She, Judy Moody, had her lucky penny.

Frank spelled *measles* with a *Z*. Rocky spelled *quesadilla,* but he forgot about the *L*s and said *Y* instead. And Jessica "A-is-for-Aardwolf" Finch spelled *bonanza.* Perfectly. *Z* and all.

Judy would rather get *measles* than have to spell *quesadilla* in a spelling *bonanza.*

Finally, Mr Todd called on Judy. She took one last look at her study sheet before getting up. Her feet felt like *cement.* Her stomach turned a *somersault.* If only she could write spelling words in *graffiti* on her hand.

That would get her nowhere but the *head teacher*'s office.

Judy stood in front of the class. Her hands started to sweat. She reached into her pocket and rubbed her lucky penny.

Please give me a lucky word, she thought to herself. *An easy-peasy word from page one of the study pages, like* berry *or* cherry *or* funny *or* bunny.

"Judy," said Mr Todd. "The word is *punctuate.*"

Punk-chew-ate! *Punctuate* was not a lucky word. *Punctuate* was not an easy-peasy page-one word. *Punctuate* was not *berry* or *cherry* or *funny* or *bunny*! Judy felt a lump in her throat. Her mouth went bone-dry as a desert. She felt cactus prickles up and down her arms.

Maybe she was coming down with a *measles bonanza*.

She looked around the room for help. Posters lined the noticeboard. Posters for grammar, spelling and ... punctuation!

Holy Macaroni! This was her lucky day after all. *Punctuate* was part of *punctuation*. All she had to do was remember to end with an *e*.

"*Punctuate.* P-U-N-C-T-U-A-T-um-E! *Punctuate.*" She let out a whoosh of air.

"Can you use it in a sentence?" asked Mr Todd.

"I'd like to punctuate the person who thought up spelling bees," said Judy.

Class 3T cracked up.

Mr Todd rolled his eyes to the ceiling. "I think we'll have to punctuate this spelling bee until tomorrow." He turned to erase the board. "Don't forget to take your study packets home, class. Pair up with a study buddy and practise, practise, practise. Our class spelling bee is in one week."

"Wowzer, Judy!" said Frank as soon as the final bell rang. "How did you know how to spell that hard word?"

"Pure luck," said Rocky. "It was right there on the noticeboard, huh, Judy? I saw you see it."

"For real? I didn't even see you see me see it," said Judy.

"You're like the luckiest person on the planet or something," said Frank.

Judy did not even say "Or something." She *was* the luckiest person ever. There was no stopping her now.

"Bye, Mr Todd," Judy said on her way out of the door. "See you in Washington DC."

"Keep up that positive attitude, Judy. I've always said you can do anything you set your mind to. Even spelling."

Judy smiled a secret smile to herself. Mr Todd did not know that she, Judy Moody, was on a lucky streak. And she planned to ride that lucky streak all the way to Washington DC.

The Bad-Luck Charm

It was one week, two study buddies (Rocky plus Frank) and three practice bees later.

Judy Moody shook her Magic 8 Ball.

"Will I win the class spelling bee?"

Reply *hazy.*

"Will I finally get to go to Washington DC?"

Ask again later.

Double drat!

"Judy?" said Dad. "Your class bee is tomorrow, isn't it? Are you up to speed on all your spelling words?"

"*Berry, furry, merry, hurry, cherry, bunny, funny,*" said Judy.

"We mean *past* page one of your spelling packet," said Mum.

Hello! Judy reached into her pocket and pulled out her lucky penny. She held it up for Mum and Dad to see.

Mum came over and put an arm around her shoulder. "Honey, I know how much you like that lucky penny. And it's fine to carry it around – for fun."

"But if you're serious about winning a spelling bee," said Dad, "you're going to have to work at it."

Mum nodded. "You're not going to win the spelling bee based on *one* lucky penny."

"In fact—" began Dad, but Judy did not want to hear it. She clomped upstairs to study before Mum and Dad could say any more bad stuff about good luck.

She took out her spelling list. She turned to the hard page. As in D-I-F-F-I-C-U-L-T.

Destiny. She closed her eyes. Des+tiny. D-E-S-T-I-N-Y. It was her own tiny *destiny* to go to Washington DC.

So far so good. Next word. *Present.* She closed her eyes again. P-R-E-S-I-D-E-N-T. The *president* lived in Washington DC. Just think. If she, Judy Moody, was lucky enough to go to DC, she just-might-maybe see the *president* himself.

Judy opened her eyes and stared at the word *present*-not-*president*. She'd practised the wrong word. It was no use.

She got out a fake-fur neon-pink rabbit's-foot keychain, three acorns, two cat's-eye marbles and one lucky stone. Seven more lucky charms!

Her mother was probably right. *One*

lucky penny was *not* enough to win a spelling bee. She would fill the pockets of her cargo trousers with tons of good-luck charms. Good luck times seven!

Judy went to sleep sure that good luck was her *destiny* for the *present.*

@ @ @

Until … the next day.

Spelling Bee day!

On the bus, Judy reached into her right shorts pocket. Empty! Of all the days to oversleep. How could she forget to wear her trousers full of lucky charms? Seven extra-sure foolproof lucky charms were in the pockets of her cargo trousers – at home on her bottom bunk. Bringing good luck to nobody, except maybe Mouse the cat.

She reached into her left pocket. Phew! Good thing she still had her lucky penny. All was not lost.

"Third-graders!" said Mr Todd when Judy got to school. "Are you ready?"

"Yes!"

"What are you ready for?"

"Spelling Bee!"

"Put away your study folders and form a line at the back of the room," said Mr Todd. "May the best speller win!"

Judy put her spelling folder away. She

never had made it past the first few words on the hard page.

All of a sudden, she did not feel so good. She was in a cherry-berry hurry-flurry to get out of the room.

"Mr Todd, may I please go to the toilet?" Judy asked.

"Quickly," said Mr Todd.

Judy speed-walked down the hall to the girl's bathroom. She did not really have to go, but she sat down on the toilet. She hummed "Twinkle, Twinkle, Little Star" to calm herself down. She recited "Tikki tikki tembo-no sa rembo-chari bari ruchi-pip peri pembo" from a story her dad used to tell her about a kid with a very long name.

Judy did not know how many minutes went by. But if she stayed away much longer, Mr Todd would send somebody to find her.

On the way back to class, she reached into her pocket to rub her lucky penny.

Holy Macaroni!

Her left pocket was empty! The lucky penny was G-O-N-E *gone!*

Judy rushed back to the girl's room. She looked around the sink. She looked on the floor. She looked you-know-where.

There, in all its copper coolness, was her lucky penny. *In the toilet!*

The upside-down horseshoe smiled up at her.

She did not have a ruler. She did not

have a Grouchy pencil. She did not have anything to fish it out with. She, Judy Moody, stuck her real-not-fake hand in the toilet! C-O-L-D *cold!* G-R-O-S-S *gross!* Yuck and double-bluck.

She fished out the lucky penny.

Judy ran to the sink and washed off the

lucky penny and her hand. With soap. Double phew! That was a close one.

Back in Room 3T, the spell-a-thon was in full swing. Judy slid into line.

Jessica Finch got the word *bamboo*. No fair! Easy-peasy. Rocky got *caboose*. Double easy-peasy. Frank got *waffle*. His favourite food!

At last it was Judy's turn. Her heart beat faster. She double-crossed her fingers and squeezed her eyes shut. *Easy word, easy word,* she wished on her lucky penny.

"The word is *Chihuahua*," said Mr Todd.

Holy Burrito!

Judy opened her eyes. *Chi-wa-wa!* That was a way-hard word. A hard word that was not *bunny* or *funny*. A NOT page-one word.

She tried to picture the word. But all she could see were pugs. Not one Chihuahua. Maybe if she started spelling, she'd get lucky.

Judy cleared her throat. "C-H-I..." *Yikes. What came next?* "H-A-W-A-I-I. *Chihuahua.*"

"Sorry," said Mr Todd. "Incorrect. But you did spell *Hawaii* nicely."

What? Judy was dumbstruck. Her feet were frozen to her spot on the floor. This could not be happening. Judy was O-U-T *out* on the first word?

"Thank you, Judy," said Mr Todd. "You may take your seat."

Judy sat down. She slumped in her chair. What in the world made her spell Hawaii? Had her lucky penny gone for-sure-and-absolute C-U-C-K-O-O?

For the rest of the spellathon, the room was a tornado of whirling, swirling words: *Mermaid. Butterscotch. Tornado.*

But Judy Moody did not seem to hear. Or see. Or notice.

Finally ... Jessica Finch was the only one left standing. What an aardwolf.

"And the winner is Jessica Finch!" said Mr Todd. "Congratulations, Jessica. You will be representing Class 3T in the Great Third-Grade Spelling Bee in Washington DC."

Everybody whooped and clapped.

Judy clapped, too. But she was not clapping on the inside.

Of all the luck! She, Judy Moody, would not be going to Washington DC. Her chances of visiting the District of Cool had just gone Down the Can. As in *toilet*.

Toilet! Of course! Her lucky penny. It must have gone kerflooey when she dropped it in the toilet. The toilet messed up its magic, jinxing her double-bad. Judy took the penny out of her pocket. The smiling horseshoe had become an upside-down frown. ROAR!

Goodbye, good-luck penny. Hello, bad-luck charm.

Uck Bluck Luck

As soon as Judy got home, she looked for a place to hide her P.U. *un*-lucky penny. She zoomed around the house. Where-o-where? Stink's room! Stink liked smelly stuff, and he was not afraid of cooties.

She looked all around. Under Stink's pillow. Perfecto! Good riddance to bad luck.

Cheese Louise. Now she had NO luck at all. If she was going to keep her good-luck streak going, she needed a brand-new, un-P.U. good-luck charm for sure.

Judy grabbed the magnifying glass from her detective kit. She ran outside. Crawling on all fours, she peered closely at the grass, searching for a four-leaf clover for what felt like an hour. Or longer.

All of a sudden, the back door banged. "Whatcha doing?" Stink asked.

"Something," she said without looking up.

"Something what?" Stink asked, nose-to-nose with the grass now, too.

"I'm looking for good luck," said Judy, still not looking up.

"I had some good luck. Just now," said Stink. He blew a bubble-gum bubble and popped it. "I found three whole pieces of Yubba Dubba gum in my desk that I didn't even know I had. Lucky, huh? The fortune in the comic says *You will soon take a trip.*"

Judy looked up. A trip! As in to Washington DC? If only *she* had got that fortune. No such luck. She went back to her search.

"Is that lucky grass or something?" Stink asked.

"Or something. If you must know, Stinker, I'm looking for a lucky four-leaf clover." So far she had found one rock, three dandelions and about ten-hundred *un*-lucky three-leaf clovers. Not one single clover with four leaves.

Not even a lucky ladybird.

"Did you know the odds of finding a four-leaf clover are like ten-thousand to one? That means you have to look through nine-thousand nine-hundred and ninety-nine three-leaf clovers to find one."

"Thanks a lot," said Judy.

"It's possible," said Stink. "A guy in Alaska found 111,060 four-leaf clovers."

"Maybe I should move to Alaska," said Judy.

Just then, something landed on Stink's arm. "Hey, a ladybird!" said Stink. "Aren't they good luck?"

Judy popped up. "Just my luck. A ladybird landed on *you*!"

"Cool! *Three* lucky things have happened to me since I got home from school," said Stink. "I found that bubble gum I didn't know I had. And now this ladybird landed on me."

"That's two things. What's the third thing?"

"The third thing was really the first thing, which is why the second and third things must have happened."

"Is this a riddle?" Judy asked.

"Look what I found under my pillow." Stink held up the lucky penny. "And I didn't even lose a tooth! It's *my* lucky penny now. That's the third lucky thing that was really the first lucky thing."

Yikes. Maybe Judy had ditched the penny too soon. "Fine. But just so you know … it's a *bad*-luck penny now."

"Is not!" Stink held it right up to his face and planted a kiss on it. *Mine o mine o mine!* he sang.

"GROSS!" yelled Judy, making an ucky-blucky face.

"What?"

"Oh, nothing," said Judy.

Stink eyed the penny suspiciously now. "Tell me."

"It's just that – the penny has cooties."

"You're just saying that," said Stink.

"Stink, do you want to know *why* it's a bad-luck penny with cooties now? Because something happened that changed the good luck to bad."

"What?"

"It went plop. It did a high-dive belly

flop. Whooo... PSSH!" Judy mimed a high dive with her hand.

"Huh?"

"The toilet, Stink. I dropped it *in the toilet*!"

"UCCCKKK! Bluck, bluck, bluck, bluck, BLUCK!" Stink let go of the penny. It flew through the air and plopped in the grass. Judy made note of where it landed.

"Good riddance to bad cooties," said Stink. "You can be in that T. P. Club all by yourself. The Toilet Penny Club."

"Ha, ha, very funny, Stink," said Judy.

Stink ran inside the house. Judy crawled across the grass and plucked the penny from the crabgrass, smiling as if she'd just picked a four-leaf clover.

She did NOT kiss the penny. She put it back in her pocket.

Just then Mum called, "Judy, can you come inside for a sec?"

Judy ran into the kitchen. Dad stood at the sink, doing dishes. Stink was eating frozen corn from a freezer bag. "What's up?"

"Mrs Finch, you know, Jessica's mother, just called."

"Uh-huh."

"You know that Jessica is going to DC for the third-grade spelling bee?"

"Uh-huh."

"And you know that she just got a pot-bellied pig for her birthday?"

"Uh-huh. PeeGee WeeGee."

"Well, Jessica would like to know if you can take care of PeeGee WeeGee while she's at the spelling bee?"

Jessica Finch, Super Speller, was going to Washington DC, District of Cooties. She, Judy Moody, would be stuck in Frog Neck *Un*-lucky Lake, Virginia, being a great big pig sitter. *Oink!*

That little piggy went to DC. This little piggy stayed home... This little piggy went roar, roar, roar all the way home.

"I don't know," said Judy.

Dad wiped his hands on the towel. "Mum and I thought you'd jump at the chance to go to Washington DC."

"Washington what? Who? Huh? Me?" Judy asked, looking from Mum to Dad.

Mum laughed. "Jessica doesn't want to leave her pig behind, since she just got him and all, so they've found a pet-friendly hotel. They're taking PeeGee with them."

"But they need a pig sitter when they're at the spelling bee. So Mum and I thought we might take you and Stink down a day early and do a little sight-seeing first," said Dad.

"For real?"

Holy Baloney! Judy Moody could not believe her this-little-piggy ears.

"So my bubble-gum fortune came true?" Stink bounced up and down on his toes. "I *am* going to take a trip soon!"

Bubble gum, schmubble gum. This

could mean only one thing: Judy's lucky penny still had some luck in it! Good thing she'd rescued it from Stink.

The Moodys were going to the District of (Not) Cooties.

"So ... what do you think?" Mum asked. "What should I tell Mrs Finch?"

"Tell her I said, 'Judy Moody, Pig Sitter, at your service!'"

The District of Cool

Road trip! The Moodys were on their way to Washington DC. Double Cool!

In the car, Judy could hardly sit still. In almost exactly one hour and twenty-seven minutes, she would be in the District of (not) Cooties!

Except it took more like four hours because of Stink.

1.) He had stop to go to the bathroom.

2.) He had to stop to buy some Yubba Dubba bubble gum.

3.) He saw a giant statue of
     a giant's head coming
     up out of the ground
     and – *POP!* – got
     bubble gum all over
     his face and hair.

4.) He had to stop to get
     de-gummed.

When at last, finally, in the end, they
got there, Judy had to wake him up. "Stink!
We're here! The District of Coolsville!"

Dad parked and they walked along
the Mall that was not a mall at all. It was
more like a park with a long reflecting
pool and tons of famous, cool stuff you
see on money. Judy saw the fancy White
House where the Big Boss of the Whole

Entire Country lived. Aka the Prez. Plus the First Lady and First Kids and First Dog.

Da-da-da Dome! Judy saw a big important building with a dome where some Big Important People decided Big Important Stuff like laws or something.

Judy saw a tall, skinny pyramid thingie called the Washington Monument. Mum said it was almost as tall as the Eiffel Tower!

Judy's eyes bugged out when she saw the real, actual statue of Abe Lincoln, called the Lincoln Memorial, just like on the back of a not-lucky penny. RARE!

"I bet James Madison, best-president-ever, stood right here," said Stink. "James Madison could have spat on this road.

James Madison could have eaten a hot dog on this bench."

"Hot dogs weren't even invented yet," said Judy.

"How do you know?" said Stink.

"I know you have James Madison on the brain," said Judy.

Dad checked his watch. "Who wants to go to the museum?"

"Is it the boring kind? Or the way-not-boring kind?" said Judy.

"Way-not-boring," said Mum, pointing to a bunch of museums that were part of the Smithsonian.

"Whoa! Check it out," Stink said, running down the pavement. "A castle!"

"Let's start there," said Dad. "It's the info centre."

"What do they have at this way-not-boring museum?" Judy asked.

"The Hope Diamond," said Mum.

"Lincoln's stovepipe hat," said Dad.

"Shrunken heads and dino poo!" said Stink.

"They do not," said Judy.

"Yah-huh. No lie," said Stink. "I saw it when I came here before with my class. Plus they have three thousand sea slugs, fifty thousand flies, and one hundred and fifteen thousand bird eggs."

"We are SO there," said Judy.

✿   ✿   ✿

Here is what she, Judy Moody, saw up-close-and-personal at the way-not-boring museum:

- Astronaut boots
- Barf bags
- Brick from the Great Wall of China
- Robber crabs (They steal forks and spoons! No lie!)
- 7 million beetles, including the endangered Northeast beach tiger beetle
- 1 million samples of dirt
- 10,000-year-old sloth dung
- President Warren G. Harding's pyjamas
- Lock of George Washington's hair (+ hairy locks of 15 more presidents)
- Way-old pack of gum

@ @ @

After the museum, they hit the gift shop. Judy used her lucky Crazy Strips money to get freeze-dried ice cream (just like the astronauts). And a book about stuff to make with duct tape.

Stink already had the James Madison 30-cm ruler, the James Madison mini statue and the James Madison friendship coin. And they were all sold out of James

Madison talking bobbleheads. So he got a plastic *un*-talking statue of Abe Lincoln.

"Abe Lincoln is my second-best president," said Stink as they walked back to the car. "See? It says eman-ci-potato at the bottom.

"Potato? Let me see," said Judy. She sounded out the word at the bottom.

"E-M-A-N-C-I-P-A-T-I-O-N. What's *emancipation*?" Judy asked Mum and Dad.

"It means to set free," said Mum.

"Lincoln set potatoes free?" Stink asked.

Mum chuckled. "No, Lincoln is famous for writing something called the Emancipation Proclamation."

"In it, he said slaves should be free," Dad added.

"Everybody knows that," said Stink.

"Speaking of Abe Lincoln," said Judy. "Will we have time to go to the Museum of Doctor Stuff? They have Abe Lincoln's skull bone there. No lie."

"Sorry, Jelly Bean," said Dad. "Mum already checked. The National Museum of Health and Medicine had a power cut. They're closed today."

"Rat fink," said Judy.

"How about the World's Almost-Biggest Chair?" Stink asked. "I didn't get to see that last time. Can we go? Can we? Can we?"

"Sure," said Dad.

"No fair. Stink gets to do his thing and my thing is closed. That stinks on ice."

"Tell you what," said Mum, checking

her map. "We can drive past the chair on our way to the Frederick Douglass House in Cedar Hill."

"Frederick Douglass! Mr Todd told us all about him for Black History Month."

"I thought you might like that," said Mum.

"Who's Frederick Douglass?" Stink asked.

"He was a great American thinker and speaker," said Dad.

"He was a slave and he escaped and fought for freedom," said Mum.

"He told President Lincoln how being a slave was really, really bad," said Judy. "And he said everybody should be able to vote. He even got in a fight with Lincoln about it. But that was like four score and seven million years ago."

Mum smiled.

"I think Mr Todd would be proud of you," said Dad.

"And now I can tell him I saw his house!"

❀   ❀   ❀

The World's Almost-Biggest Chair sat out on the pavement in front of a car park.

"Can I climb up it?" Stink asked.

"Go ahead," said Judy. "If you want to get the World's Biggest Time-Out!"

Next stop: Cedar Hill. When they got to the Frederick Douglass house, there was an orange plastic fence around it, and yellow tape that said DO NOT CROSS.

"Under construction," said Mum.

"Aw, this is closed, too?" Judy asked. Double rat fink! She should have rubbed her lucky penny.

A park ranger came out and said they were fixing up the house, and all the stuff was in storage. But they could take a tour of the grounds.

Bor-ing! Judy and Stink sat on a bummed-out bench while Mum and Dad walked around and read blah-blah-blah to each other from their guidebooks.

The flyer with the map had a lot of pictures. "Here, I'll give you the tour," said Judy. "This is a fancy bedroom. This is a fancy room where he played checkers. This is the not-so-fancy kitchen."

Stink peered at the shiny pictures. "Hey, wait. What's this?" Judy saw a picture of a little stone house with a chimney. "Stink! Follow me!"

Judy led the way to a little stone house in the back garden. Inside was a high desk with a stool. "What is it?" Stink asked as they stepped through the doorway.

"It's called the Growlery," said Judy. "This is where Frederick Douglass came to growl when he was in a bad mood."

"No. What is it for real?"

"That *is* for real, Stink. No lie. It says so right here." Judy pointed to the caption under the picture. "He had a whole house for bad moods."

"A bad mood house. Whoa," said Stink. "GRRRRRRR!" He roared like a lion.

"ROARRRRRRR!" said Judy.

Mum and Dad poked their heads into the Growlery.

"It's a house for bad moods!" said Judy.

"I see," said Dad.

"I heard," said Mum.

"We should move this to our house. For Judy!" Stink cracked himself up.

"Time to go, kids," said Dad. "We have to meet the Finches for dinner so Judy can find out about taking care of PeeGee. Then we'll check into our hotel."

"Can't we stay a little longer?" asked Stink.

"Please-pretty-please with astronaut ice cream on top?" Judy asked.

"Five minutes," said Mum.

ʖ ʖ ʖ

She, Judy Moody, was still the luckiest kid alive. How many kids got to go to the

District of Cool and see a giant giant's head, robber crabs and a 10,000-year-old ball of dung. And scream their heads off in a Bad Mood house. All in one day!

Washington was Washing*fun!*

Finch-Face Freakout

Dinnertime! The Moodys waited for Jessica Finch and her family at KaBob's Place.

Stink showed Judy the menu. "Every food here is on a stick. Hot-dog kabobs. Batter-dipped-veggie kabobs. Even fruit kabobs."

Judy was building the Washington Monument out of sugar packets. "Stink, don't shake the— Tim-ber!" said Judy, as her sugar packets came crashing down.

At last, the Finches arrived. Judy and Stink could not stop talking about Washing*fun*. They told Jessica about the Bad Mood House and the giant chair and the way-old dung.

Judy glanced all around. "Hey, where's your pig?" she asked.

"PeeGee WeeGee's in the car," said Jessica.

"He'll be OK in his kennel while we eat," said Mr Finch.

After they ordered, Mum said, "So, tomorrow's the big spelling bee, Jessica. How do you feel?"

"My tummy's doing gymnastics," said Jessica. "It's like the Olympics in there."

"Nothing a grilled-cheese kabob won't fix," said Mrs Finch.

"I could never ever spell in front of a million people," said Judy. "Even *with* my lucky penny."

Jessica Finch took out her list of spelling words. "I have to keep studying. Only seventeen hours and thirty-three minutes till Bee Time."

"Hey. Want me to quiz you?" Judy asked. "I'll be your study buddy."

"Great idea, girls," said Mum.

Judy ran her finger down the list. Jessica spelled *neighbour* and *zipper* and *alligator*. She spelled *library* and *geography*.

"Spell *shampoo banana*," said Stink.

"*Shampoo banana* is not on the spelling list, Stink."

"S-H-A-M-P-O-O B-A-N-A-N-A," said Jessica.

"Sure," said Judy, "but can you spell *berryfurrymerrycherryhoneybunnyfunny*?"

"That's like half the words on page one," Jessica said.

"I bet you can, Sweet Pea," said Mr Finch.

Jessica took a deep breath. "B-E-R-R-Y-F-U-R-R-Y-M-E-R-R-Y-C-H-E-R-R-Y-H-O-N-E-Y-B-U-N-N-Y-F-U-N-N-Y."

"As your study buddy," said Judy, "can I just say? You are *so* going to win."

"We heard Orchard Elementary has a boy named Sanjay Sharma who's really good. He may be tough to beat," said Mr Finch.

"Yes, but can he spell half the words on page one at warp speed without taking a breath?"

"Thanks," said Jessica.

At the salad bar, Jessica spelled *mushroom* and *watermelon*. She spelled *artichoke, cucumber* and *cauliflower*.

"Even the salad is on a stick!" said Jessica, showing off her plate.

"Jessica can spell the whole salad bar!" Judy told everybody at the table. She set the spelling list in her lap.

"Those are page-three words," said Jessica. "It's page four that gets me. Like *heirloom*. I keep spelling it HAIR-loom."

"Those are like *fourth*-grade words," said Judy.

When their main courses came, Stink said, "Even vegetables taste good on a stick."

"Stink would eat *camel* on a stick,"

said Judy. "Hey, Jessica? Can you spell *KABOBBLEHEAD?*"

Just then, Judy dropped her mini-meatball kabob. It landed – *SPLAT!* – right smack-dab in the middle of her lap! On her lap was not a napkin, but ... Jessica's spelling list! Page four. Judy swiped at the spelling list with her napkin.

Yikes-a-roni! Page four now had a big fat meatball smudge that would not budge. Judy flipped the list back to page one. Good thing they were done studying. She slid the list across the table towards Jessica's plate.

᠗   ᠗   ᠗

When they got to the hotel, Mum and Dad checked them in. They stood in line behind a guy with a pet iguana named Iggy. A kid walked past them in the lobby with a chinchilla on a lead.

"This is the coolest hotel ever!" said Judy.

"Check out the glass elevator," said Stink, pointing.

"It's like the Eiffel Tower."

"It's like *Charlie and the Great Glass Elevator*," said Stink. "Maybe we'll get to ride with Oompa-Loompas."

"Try to get a room on the seventh floor," Judy told her parents.

"That's where our room is!" said Jessica.

"Seven is good luck," said Judy. "Maybe that means you'll win the spelling bee!"

"Oh yeah. Don't forget I need my spell-ing list back," said Jessica.

"Spelling list?" said Judy. "I don't have your list. I thought *you* had your list."

"I don't have my list. I thought *you* had my list."

Judy shook her head no.

"We started eating. We were done spelling. So I gave it back to you." A prickle of guilt made Judy's face grow hot. She did not mention the Meatball Smudge Incident. But that's how she knew she had given the list back. She remembered wiping the smudge, flipping the list back to page one and passing it across the table to Jessica.

"What am I gonna do?" Jessica wailed.

"Judy? Is this true?" asked Mum.

"Did you forget Jessica's list at the restaurant?" asked Mrs Finch.

"I didn't forget it," said Judy. "I gave the list back to her. *She* forgot it."

Fink-Face Finch squinted her beady eyes at Judy.

"You're a bad-luck charm, Judy Moody."

"Am not!"

"If you don't want me to win" – Jessica sniffed – "just say so."

"Mum!" said Judy. "That is so not true. Honest!"

"No worries," said Mum. "Let's just call the restaurant and find out if someone found the list."

"But what if— I mean—" Jessica was tearing up, half-sobbing. "What if they threw it in the T-R-A-S-H?"

Mr Finch called KaBob's Place. Mr Finch said, "Uh-huh, uh-huh."

"Good news. We're in luck!" said Mr Finch, after he hung up the phone. "The waitress found the list on our table. They're holding it at the cash register."

"Jessica has a big day tomorrow," said Dad. "Why don't you go up to your room and relax. Judy and I will go back and get the list. We're more than happy to help, right, Judy?"

Judy half-nodded. Fink-Face Finch sure knew how to turn on the waterworks and make everybody think she had done this on purpose. It was on-top-of-spaghetti way-not-fair.

ROAR! *Where was the Growly House when you needed it?*

Just when she'd been starting to think Jessica was an UN-fink, too. She'd like to give that Jessica Finch a Shampoo Banana.

When Judy and Dad came back from KaBob's Place with the spelling list, Mum said, "Honey, take it over to Jessica. They're right across the hall in room 711."

There were exactly three things wrong with that plan.

1.) Judy still wanted to give Fink-Face
Finch a HAIRLOOM full of banana.

2.) There was still that big fat kabob blob
    smack in the middle of page four.
3.) Jessica A. Freakazoid would go nuts
    when she saw the blob.

"Mum, I might have spilled a kabob on page four. Do you think she'll notice?"

"Let me see." Stink took a look at the list. "Oh, she'll notice. This looks like it was on the *Titanic – after* it sank."

"Stink, you're not helping," said Dad.

Judy snatched the list out of Stink's hand. She stomped across the hall. She stood outside the door and rubbed her lucky penny. *Don't be mad. Don't be mad.* Maybe she'd get lucky and Jessica would not turn to page four.

Judy knocked on the door. "Room service!" she called.

Jessica opened the door. Mr and Mrs Finch were watching TV. PeeGee WeeGee was curled up asleep on Jessica's bed.

"Here's your list." Judy handed it over.

The list was wrinkled. The list was crinkled. The list looked like it had just survived a food fight. Or a tsunami. Or a tsunami food fight.

Jessica started to flip through the pages. Some luck.

"I may have spilled

115

a little something on page four," Judy blurted.

"A *little* something?" Jessica wailed. "I can't read half these words. What if the winning word is under this smudge? I could lose the whole spelling bee because of this. Which means our whole class could lose. Our whole school could lose."

"I'm VERY BERRY FURRY MERRY CHERRY HONEY BUNNY FUNNY sorry."

"Why do you have to Judy-Moody-ruin everything?" Jessica said, sighing.

"I didn't do it on purpose," Judy said in a low voice.

Jessica crossed her arms. She dug her foot into the carpet.

Judy's ears burned. Her mouth felt like sand. "Go ahead. Don't believe me," she croaked. "I'm going to emancipate from you if that'll make you happy."

"Huh?"

"Emancipate. It means to *set free*. I'm free now. Free from being your Study Buddy. And you're free, too. Free from my bad luck."

Jessica's mouth hung open. "What are you saying? I don't get it."

"Then let me spell it out. E-M-A-N-C-I-P-A-T-E." Judy stormed across the hall. "Do you want me to use it in a sentence?"

Judy Moody, Pig Sitter

The next morning, Judy peered through the peephole in the hotel door that looked out into the hall. All she could see was nothing. All she could hear was the slam of the door from last night after she got mad at Jessica.

Judy sat on the edge of the foldout bed. She, Judy Moody, was a cruddy Study

Buddy. Now Jessica would think she was a crummy pig sitter, too. She twirled and twisted her hair until it made a big fat knot. Ouch.

Knock knock!

She leapt up and ran to the door.

Jessica Finch. Plus one potbellied piggy on a lead!

Judy forgot she was still mad. "PeeGee WeeGee!" she said, throwing open the door. Judy bent down to scratch the piggy's ears. PeeGee WeeGee snuffled the carpet. PeeGee WeeGee turned in circles. PeeGee WeeGee curled his tail. "At least somebody's happy to see me."

Jessica had her hair in a special pig-tail. And she was wearing a pink skirt and a T-shirt that had a picture of a pig. It said I'M WITH HIM. "I know you want to *emancipate* from me and everything," said Jessica. "But I still need you to baby-sit my pig."

"I thought *you* wanted to emancipate from *me*, too," said Judy.

"I did. I do. But you made a piggy promise," said Jessica. "Besides, I can't take a *pig* to a spelling *bee*." Jessica snorted and laughed like a hyena.

Once upon a lucky penny, Judy had wanted to be in the spelling bee herself. But now she was happy to be a pig sitter. "C'mon, PeeGee WeeGee," said Judy, taking the lead. "We are going to have way more fun than any old spelling bee,

aren't we?" PeeGee WeeGee snuffled her
messy hair.

Stink came to the door. He scratched
under the piggy's ears. "Remember me?"

"I call him P.G. for short," said Jessica.
"Hold on." She ran back to her room.
She came back carrying boatloads of pig
stuff.

"Here's his water dish. Make sure he
has fresh water at all times."

"Check," said Judy.

"Here's his busy ball. Pig pellets come
out, in case he gets hungry. I forgot Binky,
his favourite stuffed animal. But here's
his favourite blankie if he wants to take
a nap."

"Check," said Judy.

"He likes this pillow, too." Jessica handed Judy a pillowcase filled with beans. "He curls up on it. Oh, and this is special shampoo in case you want to give him a bath."

"Does he have a favourite song, like 'On Top of Spaghetti'?" Judy teased.

"Oops! I almost forgot." Jessica ran away and came back waving a piece of notebook paper. "His favourite song is 'This Little Piggy' but these are the words he likes better. I wrote them out for you."

Judy looked at Stink and made the cuckoo sign.

Mr and Mrs Finch came out of their room across the hall. "Time to go, honey," said Mrs Finch. "The spelling bee starts in one hour. Judy, do you and Stink have everything you need?"

Judy nodded. "I'm good with pigs," she said.

The Moodys stepped out into the hall. "Just do your best today," Mum said to Jessica. "You're going to be great."

"Class 3T will be proud," said Dad.

"Thanks," said Jessica. "Wish me luck."

"Break a leg," said Stink.

"I hope not!" said Jessica.

"Well, then, break a pigtail," said Judy. She cracked herself up.

Jessica leaned down to give P.G. one more hug. "Don't let P.G. eat candy bars," she called over her shoulder.

"Say hi to Mr Todd!" Judy called back.

"Oh, and TV kind of freaks him out," Jessica added, "unless it's the movie *Babe*."

"Don't worry about P.G.," said Mum. "The kids will take good care of him."

As soon as Jessica and her parents were gone, Judy threw her hands in the air and yelled, "Let's have a piggy party!"

"Kids," said Dad. "Keep P.G. in here. Mum and I will be right outside on the balcony if you need us."

"Sure," said Judy.

PeeGee WeeGee stood in a corner, shaking.

"What's wrong with him?" Stink asked.

"I think he's scared," said Judy.

P.G. raised one eyebrow and grunted. All of a sudden, Judy smelled a terrible, no-good, very bad smell.

"Stink-*er*!" said Judy.

"It wasn't me," said Stink. "It was the pig. I read in the *P* encyclopedia that pigs can let go an awful smell when they're scared."

Judy cracked open a window. "We should call him P.U." Judy said. "Not P.G."

Judy and Stink sat on the floor across from each other and rolled the busy ball back and forth between them. After a few minutes, P.G. quietened down and stopped quivering.

"Try rolling the ball to him now, Stink."

P.G. raised his ears. He chased after the ball. The ball rolled under the bed.

P.G. dived in after it and came out the other side.

"Good boy, P.G.," said Judy. She scooped up the ball and shook it. "Little pellets are supposed to fall out for him to eat."

"Do you think he's hungry?" asked Stink.

"Pigs are always hungry," said Judy.

Stink ate some crisps from a bag. P.G. went bananas, tearing around the room.

"Stink! He can't have candy. Put that away! You're making him all cuckoo."

"It's not candy. It's crisps."

"Whatever. The noisy bag sound is driving him crazy."

"He wants something in your suit-case," said Stink. P.G. had Judy's polka-dot kneesock in his mouth.

"P. G.! Give that back!" said Judy. "You are all nose, you know that?"

"Look," said Stink. "He's trying to open the mini fridge!"

Judy picked up the phone and pressed a button. "Room service?" she asked. "Do you have any pig food?"

Judy listened. "Uh-huh. Uh-huh." She nodded. "Cottage cheese? Sounds good. Yoghurt? Sounds healthy." She nodded some more. "Thanks!"

"I know," said Judy. "Let's give P.G. a bath while we wait for the pig food."

Judy filled the tub with a little bit of warm water. "And now, for some piggy shampoo." She made the water sudsy, like a bubble bath. "In you go," she said.

P.G. kicked. P.G. splashed. P.G. jumped. "Look! He loves it," said Judy.

"Too bad we don't have a rubber ducky. I mean rubber *piggy*," said Stink.

"Stink, squeeze some shampoo on him and I'll rub it in." Stink ran to get the shampoo bottle.

"Scrub-a-dub-dubby, P.G. loves the tubby," Judy sang. P.G. snorted and squealed.

"That's not one of the songs he likes," said Stink.

"This little piggy went to DC..." Judy sang.

She rinsed him off. "There. Squeaky clean," she said. She tried to lift him out of the tub, but P.G. was all wet and wiggly. Soapy and squiggly.

"Help, Stink. Grab a towel. He's super slippery."

Stink came over and held out the towel.

Judy picked up the piglet. That pig was extra squiggly. That pig was extra wiggly.

"Mr Piggle Wiggle," said Judy. Before she could get P.G. into the towel, that little piggy squiggled and wiggled right out of Judy's arms.

That little piggy bolted right out of the bathroom. P.G. ran out into the front room. He ran right out of the door and into the hall.

"Who left the door open?" Judy called.

Judy ran after the pig. Stink ran after Judy, still holding the towel. P.G. snorted and squealed and bumped into walls. They chased that pig down the fancy carpet past paintings of cherry blossoms. They chased that pig past a calico cat with a tiara. They chased that pig to the big red EXIT sign.

"PeeGee WeeGee! Come back here!" Judy called.

Ding! Judy heard a bell. *OH NO!*

E-L-E-V-A-T-O-R! Elevator!

"Hurry, Stink! We have to get him before he goes in the— PEEGEE WEEGEE! NOooooo!"

P.G. was in the elevator!

Whoosh! The doors closed shut. P.G. was riding the elevator!

"Stink!" cried Judy. "Why didn't you grab him with the towel?"

"Are you kidding? Wet pigs are as slippery as greased lightning. And fast. We'd better go and tell Mum and Dad what happened."

"I'm telling Mum and Dad," said Judy, "when pigs fly!"

"But maybe they can put out a pig alert in the hotel or something."

"Or something!" Judy looked at the numbers above the elevator door. Up, up, up it went. "C'mon, Stink. He's going up. We have to catch him before—"

Stink pointed. "Now he's coming back down! The elevator is probably going all the way to the lobby!"

"I've got it!" said Judy. "The stairs!"

Judy and Stink pushed through the door to the stairwell. They ran down one-two-three flights of stairs. They ran down four-five-six flights of stairs.

When they got to the bottom, Judy

bent over, breathing hard. "Why did we have to get a room on the seventh floor?" Judy asked.

"Because you said seven is a lucky number," said Stink.

"Well, it sure turned out to be UN-lucky," said Judy.

They opened the door on to a hallway and turned a corner to reach the lobby.

The lobby was empty. Pigless. All the elevator doors were closed.

No sign of a pig anywhere. Not one hair. Not even a pig tail.

Pig in the City

"He's not here!" Judy cried. "What are we going to do?"

She, Judy Moody, had all the luck. *NOT.* P.G. was L-O-S-T *lost.*

"Maybe he got off on another floor," said Stink.

Ding! Just then, an elevator door opened. Judy and Stink rushed over and peered inside. A guy in a bathrobe and slippers stepped out.

"Have you seen a pig?" Judy asked the guy. "He's about this big, pinkish, with a black spot on his tail. He answers to the name PeeGee WeeGee or just P.G.?"

"Sorry. My ride was pig-free," said the guy, heading for the pool.

Ding! Another elevator landed. Only a grey-haired lady with an umbrella stepped out.

"He's got to be around here somewhere," said Judy. "C'mon, Stinker. Think like a pig."

"I'm hungry," said Stink.

"Not now, Stink."

"But you told me to think like a pig.

Pigs are always hungry." Stink cupped his hand to his mouth. "Mar-co!" he called.

"Oink-o," Judy called back.

"It's *Polo*," said Stink.

"Um, Stink, I hate to tell you, but pigs can't say 'Polo.'"

"Oh. Yeah."

Judy slumped to the floor. It was no use. Her lucky penny must be deader than a toenail. O-U-T *out* of good luck. All it seemed to bring now was the other kind. B-A-D luck.

"C'mon, Stink. If you were a pig in a big hotel, where would you go?"

"To the piggy bank?" Stink teased.

"Get serious."

"OK, I'd ride piggyback on one of those wheelie carts all the way down to the pool. Then I'd climb up the high dive and—"

"When pigs fly!" said Judy. Wait a second. *Fly?* She looked up. Of course! The glass elevator. "Follow me!"

Judy and Stink stood smack-dab in the centre of the lobby. They looked up, up, up at the fancy glass elevator. "Is that who I think it is?" Stink asked.

It was not an iguana named Iggy. It was not a chinchilla. It was not an Oompa-Loompa. It was a little piggy running in circles around the inside of the glass elevator.

"P.G.!" called Judy. *Hurry up! Hurry up!* she willed the elevator. "Why does that thing have to take so long?"

Ding! At last, the elevator landed and the door opened. P.G. was chasing his tail and kicking up his pig's feet.

"Hold the door open," Judy told Stink. She talked baby talk to P.G. "Who's a bad little piggy? You are. Yes you are. Coo, coo, coo."

"*You're* cuckoo," said Stink.

Just then, P.G. bolted out of the elevator door, away from Judy and past Stink. *Oink! Oink! Snort!* He ran squealing and grunting, slipping and sliding across the marble lobby floor. He ran over to a potted tree in the lobby and snuffled in the dirt.

"Dirt! He misses dirt!" said Stink.

Pshoo! P.G. sneezed and shook his ears. He ran in circles around the fountain in the lobby.

"P.G.! No!" said Judy, but it was too late. *Ker-splash!* P.G. bounded right in.

"Towel time," said Judy, taking the towel from Stink. "OK. I'm going to sneak up behind him and grab him." Tiptoe … tiptoe … tiptoe … *pounce!*

"Gotcha!" said Judy. She scooped P.G. up in the towel and snuggled him close. "P.G., what were you thinking? You already had a bath, you nutty pig."

Judy, Stink and P.G. got back into the

elevator. Stink pressed the button for seven. "Going up!" he called.

"You had us worried there, P.G.," said Judy. "Yes you did." She held P.G. in the air and rubbed noses with him. "Gimme a kiss!" she cooed.

When they got back, Dad poked his head into the room. "Where were you two?"

"Um, we just took P.G. for a ride in the elevator," said Judy. "No biggie."

"Next time, *ask* before you leave this room," said Mum. "Both of you."

"And who ordered all this cottage cheese?" asked Dad.

"We did. It's for P.G.," said Judy. *Snarf!* P.G. was already helping himself.

All right. I have to make a call and check in with Grandma Lou. We'll be in here if you need us," said Mum.

When P.G. was done snarfing his food, he hopped up on the bed and curled up on his special pillow. Judy wrapped him in his favourite blankie, where he snuggled with Blue Monkey. *"This little piggy rode an elevator,"* Judy sang softly.

Stink flipped on the TV. P.G. shook his head till his ears flapped and backed away.

"Stink! TV freaks him out, and I just got him to settle down."

"Sorry," said Stink. He hit the mute button, flipping through channels.

"Remember, P.G.," Judy whispered.

"No squealing on us when Jessica gets back, OK? The elevator ride? That's our little secret. Shake on it?" Judy picked up his right hoof and shook.

"Hey, look what's on!" Stink cried. "The sequel to his favourite movie. *Babe: Pig in the City!*"

"You are one lucky-ducky pig," Judy told P.G. She cuddled up with him to watch the movie. Stink turned up the sound.

"And there's Farmer Hoggett," said Judy. "He got hurt. And now Babe has to try to save the farm." They all three watched the movie. Judy and Stink laughed. "See? Babe got to stay in a hotel, too. Just like you."

"*Mmmph!*" P.G. snorted.

"Look. He's getting sleepy," said Stink.

"He's had a big day," said Judy. "He's P.G.: Pig in the City."

E-M-A-N-C-I-P-A-T-E

Zzzzz. At last, PeeGee WeeGee started to snooze. *Snurf!*

"Phew. We lucked out. He fell asleep. Doesn't he look all cute when he's sleeping?" Judy whispered.

"His eyes are moving. I think he's dreaming," said Stink.

"Visions of cottage cheese are dancing in his head," said Judy.

"Visions of *elevators*," said Stink.

"Shh!" Judy warned. Jessica Finch

could be right outside that door. It was almost four. Jessica might be coming back any minute. "No squealing about the ride on the You-Know-What," said Judy, putting her finger to her lips.

Knock knock!

Judy jumped up and opened the door. Sure enough, it was Jessica Finch. And she had a bee painted on her face. A *spelling* bee.

"How did the spelling bee—" Judy started to ask, but Jessica ran over to P.G. "Don't wake him up. I just got him—"

Too late. Jessica had already scooped P.G. up in her arms and was giving him hugs and kisses. "P.G.!" she said. "I missed you, you little pig face."

"PeeGee WeeGee!" squealed P.G. He curled his tail.

"Aw, you missed me, too, didn't you, little guy?" Jessica cooed.

Mr and Mrs Finch came up behind Jessica. They peered inside. The Moodys' hotel room was a mess. The bed was a tornado. Socks and shoes littered the floor. Trays with empty bowls of cottage cheese were here, there and everywhere.

"What happened here?" Mr Finch asked.

"This place is a pigsty!" said Jessica, cackling.

"Duh!" said Judy. "He's *your* pig. You know how he is."

"I'm afraid we do," said Mrs Finch.

Mum and Dad came out of the other room when they heard the commotion.

"The kids really had a fun time with P.G.," said Dad.

"We gave P.G. a bath," said Stink.

"And I taught him to give kisses," said Judy.

"And P.G. didn't escape or ride the elevator or anything," said Stink.

Judy gave Stink the stink-eye. "Squealer!" she muttered under her breath. She quick-changed the subject. "Hurry up, Jessica. Tell us what happened at the spelling bee."

"It was fine."

"Fine?" Judy screeched. "That's it?" Judy wagged her finger at Jessica. "Wait a second. I get it. It's OK if you didn't win, you know."

"Yeah, but, OK, um … I did win."

"You WON?" said Judy. "As in *won?* As in beat everybody? Even Sanjay Sharma? As in Class 3T and Virginia Dare School takes home the trophy for The Great Third-Grade Spelling Bee?"

Jessica nodded.

"See, told you you'd win! Even though I kabobbed your spelling list."

"Can you believe it? Our girl won," said Mr Finch.

"We're so proud of her," said Mrs Finch.

"Congratulations, Jessica!" said Mum.

"Way to go!" said Dad.

"Where's the trophy?" Stink asked.

"Then I don't get it," said Judy. "Why are you acting weird?"

"I'm not acting weird," said Jessica.

"Yes you are. You should be going crazy and running laps around the room and screaming 'I won, I won' and jumping up and down on furniture and stuff."

"Go ahead, honey. Tell us all about it," said Mum.

"Well, first I spelled *cartoon* and *nightmare*."

"Easy-peasy," said Judy. "For you, I mean."

"Then it got harder. I got flip-flops in my stomach when they said *unbelievable* because I couldn't remember if it was *I* before *E* or *E* before *I*."

"Or *E-I-E-I-O*," said Stink.

Everybody laughed.

"Then it got down to just me and Sanjay. I thought for sure he was going to win. I was so nervous my teeth were chattering like it was the middle of winter."

"What word did you win with?" Judy asked.

"Was it *titanic*?" Stink asked.

"Was it *gargantuan*?" Judy asked. "I bet it was *gargantuan*."

"Was it *president*?" Stink asked. "No wait, was it *jawbreaker*? It was *jawbreaker*, wasn't it?"

Jessica shrugged.

Mr Finch said, "Her mother and I were worried because it wasn't on any of the lists."

"We still don't know how she knew it," said Mrs Finch.

Jessica's pigtail bounced as she looked from her mum to her dad.

"Go ahead. Tell them your word, sweetheart," said Mrs Finch.

Jessica dug her shoe into the carpet. She whispered something Judy couldn't quite hear.

Judy leapt up. "What? Did you say —"

"Emancipate," said Jessica, a little louder. "OK? Are you happy? The word was *EMANCIPATE*!"

"*Emancipate!*" Judy cried. She could not help cracking up.

"Hey!" Stink ran over and grabbed Abe Lincoln. "That's the word on my second-favourite-president statue. I just got it yesterday."

"Same-same!" said Judy. "Good thing Jessica didn't spell *eman-ci-potato*."

"What a coincidence," said Dad.

"It's an UNBELIEVABLE co-inky-dink. Rare!" said Judy.

"You're on a lucky strike, Jessica," said Stink. "Like Judy."

"*Streak*," said Judy. "Lucky *streak*."

"Did you see it on my statue and that's how you knew?" said Stink. "So I helped you win?"

"Actually," Jessica admitted, "it was Judy."

"It was me who said you, Jessica Finch, can spell even fifth-grade words. In fact, I bet you could spell the whole entire dictionary!"

"Thanks," said Jessica. "Sorry I was such an aardvark."

"Aardwolf," said Judy.

"Whatever. I was just so nervous and worried about the spelling bee—"

"It's OK. Sorry I was such a meatball. I kabobbed your spelling list. Right over the important words, too."

"*Meatball* was one of the spelling-bee words!" said Jessica.

"No way!" said Judy.

"Hey, I have an idea," said Dad. "Let's emancipate ourselves from this hotel and go get some ice cream at Pitango to celebrate. What do you say?"

"Then can we go to the Old Post Office?" asked Judy. "They have a bell tower and you can climb up it and see way far away."

"I read that the clock tower has some of the best views of the city," said Mum.

"Great idea!" said Mr Finch.

Mrs Finch nodded.

"P.G. likes ice cream," said Jessica.

"I scream, you scream, we all scream for ice cream," sang Stink, leading the way.

@ @ @

The next morning, it was time to head home. Outside on the pavement in front of the hotel, the Moodys said goodbye to the Finches for what seemed like an hour. Bor-ing.

At last, the Finches' car pulled away. Judy ran down the pavement all the way to the kerb, waving and blowing kisses to P.G.

When the car was out of sight, Judy reached into her pocket to make a new wish on her lucky penny.

What! No penny?

She reached down deeper. Fooey Louie. She reached into every corner, but all she got was lint. She checked all her other pockets. Twice.

She spun around, looking here, there and everywhere. She checked the cracks in the pavement. She even searched her shoe.

No luck. The lucky penny was nowhere.
She checked her pocket one last time.
That's when she found it.

A hole!

Her lucky penny was GFG. Gone For Good. Emancipated. Set free. Was losing a lucky penny bad luck? What if she never had good luck again?

All of a sudden, a flashing light at the intersection caught her eye. Two police cars pulled up, stopping traffic.

Judy squinted down the street, into the bright light. Just then, she thought she saw— Could it be? Were her eyes playing tricks on her? *No!*

"Guys! Guys!" she yelled down the road, trying to get her family's attention. Judy rushed back to the car, banging on the window to get Mum and Stink's attention. Dad had his head in the boot, wrestling with the luggage.

Judy jumped up and down, pointing and stabbing the air. "It's him! For real! Did you see? Did you?"

"Who him?" asked Stink. He scrambled out of the car, climbed up on a bench and peered down the street. "All I see are a bunch of black cars."

"*Secret agent* black cars," said Judy. "It was him! The present. I mean president. He just jogged down that cross street. No lie!"

"Looks like the president's motorcade," said Dad.

"He must be out exercising," said Mum.

"I can't believe I missed it!" Stink told

Judy. "You saw a for-real president. No fair. You have all the luck."

"But I don't—" Judy started to say, thinking about losing her lucky penny.

Hey, wait just a lucky-ducky minute! She did have good luck without her lucky penny. Cool-o-roonie!

❧ ❧ ❧

As they pulled away, Judy gazed out of the back window of the car until the Washington Monument was nothing but a teeny tiny dot. A speck on the horizon.

She waved goodbye to the District of Cool.

She, Judy Moody, was a VERY BERRY FURRY MERRY FUNNY BUNNY LUCKY DUCKY. She had got to go on a runaway pig adventure, help win the Great Third-Grade Spelling Bee and even become real friends with Jessica Finch.

And she'd got a present. The present of seeing the president!

10 Things
You May Not
Know About
Megan McDonald

10. The first story Megan ever got published (in the fifth grade) was about a pencil sharpener.

9. She read the biography of Virginia Dare so many times at her school library that the librarian had to ask her to give somebody else a chance.

8. She had to be a boring-old pilgrim every year for Halloween because she has four older sisters, who kept passing their pilgrim costumes down to her.

7. Her favourite board game is the Game of Life.

6. She is a member of the Ice-Cream-for-Life Club at Screamin' Mimi's in her hometown of Sebastopol, California, USA.

5. She has a Band-Aid collection to rival Judy Moody's, including bacon-scented Band-Aids.

4. She owns a jawbreaker that is bigger than a baseball, which she will never, ever eat.

3. Like Stink, she had a pet newt that slipped down the drain when she was his age.

2. She often starts a book by scribbling on a napkin.

1. And the number-one thing you may not know about Megan McDonald is: she was once the opening act for the World's Biggest Cupcake!

10 Things
You May Not
Know About
Peter H. Reynolds

10. He has a twin brother, Paul. Paul was born first, fourteen minutes before Peter decided to arrive.

9. Peter is part owner of a children's book and toy shop called the Blue Bunny in the Massachusetts town where he lives.

8. Peter has a son named Henry Rocket.

7. His mother is from England; his father is from Argentina.

6. He made his first animated film at the age of twelve.

5. He sometimes paints with tea instead of water – whatever's handy!

4. He keeps a sketch pad and pen on his bedside table. That way, if an idea hits him in the middle of the night, he can jot it down immediately.

3. His favourite candy is a tie between peanut-butter cups and chocolate-covered raisins (same as Megan McDonald!).

2. One of his favourite books growing up was *The Tall Book of Make-Believe* by Jane Werner, illustrated by Garth Williams.

1. And the number-one thing you may not know about Peter H. Reynolds is: he shares a birthday with James Madison, Stink's favourite president!

Have you read them all?

Judy and Stink are starring together!

Judy Moody & Stink
The Holly Joliday

Judy Moody & Stink
The Mad, Mad, Mad, Mad Treasure Hunt

In full colour!

Be sure to check out Stink's adventures!

DOUBLE RARE!

Check out Judy Moody's new interactive website at:

www.judymoody.com

Just some of its cool features:

- ◉ The Ultimate Judy Moody Fan Quiz

- ◉ All-new interactive games and a Mood Meter

- ◉ All you need to know about the best-ever Judy Moody Fan Club

- ◉ Totally awesome T.P. Club info!

- ◉ Digital downloads

Pssst! Go to www.stinkmoody.com to find out more about me, Stink!

The Sisters Club

Dive into the real-life ups and downs of sisterhood with the series inspired by Megan McDonald's own life growing up as the youngest of five sisters!